JUST A BIG STORM

BY MERCER MAYER

To all the critters who experienced the big storm of 2011!

HARPER FESTIVAL

An Imprint of HarperCollins*Publishers*

HarperFestival is an imprint of HarperCollins Publishers.

Manufactured in China.
For information address HarperCollins Children's Books, a division of HarperCollins Publishers, 10 East 53rd Street, New York, NY 10022.
Library of Congress catalog card number: 2012942430
ISBN: 978-0-06-147804-8
Typography by Sean Boggs
12 13 14 15 16   SCP   10 9 8 7 6 5 4 3 2 1

❖

First Edition

A Big Tuna Trading Company, LLC/J.R. Sansevere Book
www.harpercollinschildrens.com   www.littlecritter.com

A storm was coming. We saw dark clouds and lightning in the distance.

"Let's check the weather channel," said Mom.
The weather critter said, "A big storm with lightning,
rain, and hail will pass right over Critterville."

"We better get ready for anything," Dad said. "We may lose power." Dad checked all the flashlights.

Little Sister and I got water in buckets for the toilet.

We put up a sign that read, "Remember: Pour water in tank before you flush."

We filled up pots at the sink for drinking water.
We put a sign on the fridge: "Do not open."

Then we rescued stuff from our yard.
The wind began to blow. It blew harder and
harder. It began to rain, too.

I saw our neighbor's garbage can fly
right past our window.

Suddenly, the power went out. It was getting
dark and we couldn't turn on a light.

Mom and Dad got out our battery-powered lanterns, and everyone had their very own flashlight.

The wind was cold, so Dad built
a fire in the woodstove. We made
knots out of newspaper to start
the fire.

We found an old phone in the closet and plugged it into the wall. Did you know old phones work sometimes when you have no power?

I called some of my friends. They didn't have any power either. I asked Mom and Dad if I could have everyone come over for a sleepover.

Mom and Dad said, "No."
That didn't seem fair.

We baked potatoes in the woodstove and made grilled cheese with a pie iron. I was careful and didn't touch the hot stove.

We played board games by lantern
light.

"This is just like camping," I said.

We got sleeping bags and all slept on the
living room floor. Dad told ghost stories.

There was lots of thunder and lightning. I wasn't scared. I snuggled real close to Mom, just in case.

We couldn't sleep.
Mom read a book to us.
Dad fell asleep first.

When we woke up, our power was back on.
We saw the power company critters
working on the electrical poles.
That was neat.

I was sad that it was all over, but Mom and Dad were happy. They said they wanted to take showers. Why would they want to do that?

Our phone rang. It was Grandma and Grandpa.
They were worried about us.

"Grandma, it wasn't so bad," I said.
"It was just a big storm."